Becci Murray

D0314304

GRANNy GOT A sprout

STUCK UP HER SNEEZER

For Jo Birks
with love for being a wonderful nan

Copyright of text and illustrations © Becci Murray 2021

All rights reserved. No part of this book may be reproduced or used in any
manner without written permission of the copyright owner except for the use of
quotations in a book review.

ISBN: 978-1-913944-16-2

Published by Llama House Children's Books

Granny got a

sprout

stuck up her sneezer,

Eating lunch at our house Christmas Day.

First she tried to pull it with the tweezers,

Then suddenly we heard poor Granny say...

proper
stuck
sprout

There's a

sprout

stuck up the nostril of my sneezer!

It somehow found its way inside my snout.

There's dinner up my nose,
How it got there, no-one knows,

Oh, won't someone find a way to get it out?

Grandpa whipped a **CARROT** from his plate.

He pushed the carrot in then pulled it straight,
As Granny gave a rather startled shout...

There's a

CARROT

up the nostril of my sneezer!

It somehow found its way inside my snout.

Your grandpa is a wally,
He's completely off his trolley,

Oh, won't someone find a way to get it out?

Mother snatched a **TURNIP** from the table.

I'll poke it free with **THIS!** my mum declared.

Mum knows best (usually)

She shoved it in as hard as she was able,

As Granny almost toppled off her chair...

There's a

TURNIP

up the nostril of my sneezer!

It somehow found its way inside my snout.

Your mother put a root,
In my unsuspecting snoot,

Oh, won't someone find a way to get it out?

Father grabbed his biggest **ROAST POTATO.**

I'll use **THIS SPUD** to shift it! he exclaimed.

an actual living genius (maybe)

He spun it like a tiny spud tornado,

And Granny started wailing once again...

There's a

TATER

up the nostril of my sneezer!

It somehow found its way inside my snout.

Your father is a fool,
He's a danger to us all,

Oh, won't someone find a way to get it out?

Auntie seized a **BIG OLD TRAY OF STUFFING.**

I'll wrench it out with **THIS!** she boldly said,

super-strong
stuffing-lifter

And with a sigh of, "Right then, here goes nothing,"
She aimed the plate of mince at Granny's head...

There's a

BIG OLD TRAY OF STUFFING

up my sneezer!

It somehow found its way inside my snout.

Your auntie tried to prod it,
With a plate of seasoned sausage,

Oh, won't someone find a way to get it out?

Uncle heaved the **TURKEY** from its platter.

We need a **BIGGER** lever! he proclaimed.

Worst idea EVER!

He threw the giant bird directly at her,

As Granny tossed her head back and exclaimed...

There's a

TURKEY

up the nostril of my sneezer!

It somehow found its way inside my snout.

Your uncle took a chance,
With a bird the size of France,

Oh, won't someone find a way to get it out?

Everyone went **ABSOLUTELY**

Dad Zombie

Mum's startled cod-fish impression

CRAZY!

"Don't worry, Gran!" I called across the plates,

And reaching past the parsnips and the gravy...

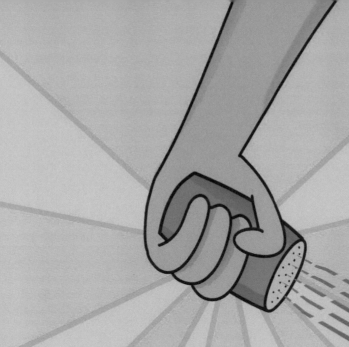

I SHOOK A CLOUD OF PEPPER IN HER FACE!

Gran's not having a good day (neither is the turkey)

ACHOO!
A turkey shot out from her sniffer!

ACHOO!
A tray of stuffing followed next!

ACHOO!
A tater hit Dad in the kisser!

ACHOO!
A turnip shattered Auntie's specs!

ACHOO! A carrot hurtled from her nozzle,

And took the head off Mother's Christmas rose,

As with a final **ACHOO!** from her schnozzle,

At last the sprout came out of Granny's nose.

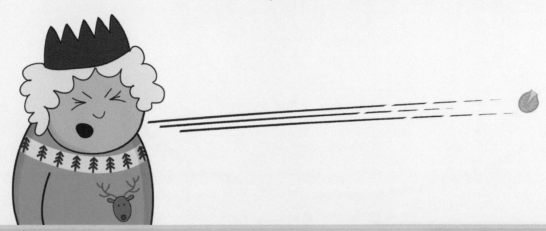

Gran's
happy-bunny
face

The hilarious series of gran-tastic catastrophes - collect them all!

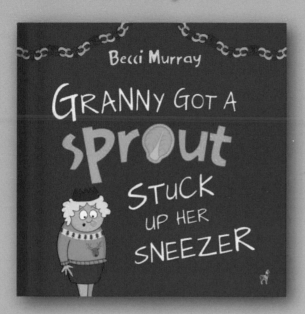

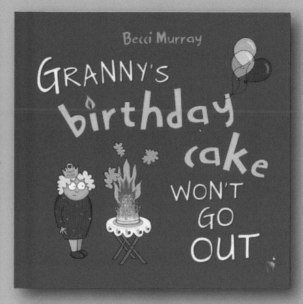

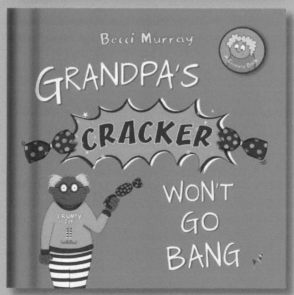

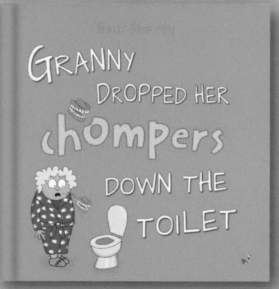

www.llamahousebooks.com

Becci Murray
(author) →

Becci Murray is a proudly
independent author from
Gloucestershire. She previously wrote
for children's television and is the
creator of the ever-growing Granny
book series.

If you enjoyed Granny Got a Sprout
Stuck Up Her Sneezer, please
consider leaving a review wherever
you purchased the book to help other
young readers discover the story.

www.llamahousebooks.com